THIS BOOK IS DEDICATED TO MY WIFE, GAIL, FOR LAUGHING AT ALL THE RIGHT TIMES.
—B.P.B.

Library of Congress Cataloging-in-Publication Data

Brodt, Burton P.
Four little old men: a (mostly) true tale from a small Cajun town / Burton P. Brodt; illustrated by Luc Melanson.
p. cm.
Summary: In a small town on the Mississippi River, four men too old to work anymore begin playing cards
together, and as the game goes on over months, they continually improve the place where they play.
ISBN 1-4027-2006-8
[1. Old age—Fiction. 2. Cajuns—Fiction. 3. Card games—Fiction. 4. Contentment—Fiction.
5. Louisiana—Fiction.] I. Melanson, Luc, ill. II. Title.
PZ7.B78614Fo 2005   [Fic]—dc22   2005008799

2 4 6 8 10 9 7 5 3 1

Published by Sterling Publishing Co., Inc.
387 Park Avenue South, New York, NY 10016
Text copyright © 2005 by Burton P. Brodt
Illustrations copyright © 2005 by Luc Melanson
Designed by Randall Heath
Distributed in Canada by Sterling Publishing
c/o Canadian Manda Group, 165 Dufferin Street
Toronto, Ontario, Canada M6K 3H6
Distributed in Great Britain and Europe by Chris Lloyd at Orca Book
Services, Stanley House, Fleets Lane, Poole BH15 3AJ, England
Distributed in Australia by Capricorn Link (Australia) Pty. Ltd.
P.O. Box 704, Windsor, NSW 2756, Australia

Printed in China

Sterling ISBN 1-4027-2006-8

For information about custom editions, special sales, premium and
corporate purchases, please contact Sterling Special Sales
Department at 800-805-5489 or specialsales@sterlingpub.com.

FOUR LITTLE OLD MEN

A (Mostly) True Tale from a Small Cajun Town

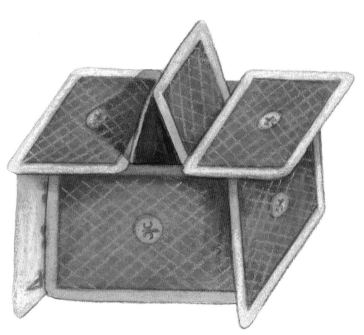

BURTON P. BRODT   ILLUSTRATED BY LUC MELANSON

STERLING PUBLISHING CO., INC.
NEW YORK

(THIS IS A TRUE STORY, MOSTLY.)

Once upon a time in Louisiana, in a small Cajun town nestled against the Mississippi River, there lived four little old men. They were so old that they didn't work anymore. No one expected them to, or even wanted them to, because whatever work they did, they tended to mess it up. So the four little old men did a lot of rocking, back and forth, back and forth, on their front porches. And as they rocked, they watched the cars and trucks traveling along the Great River Road (which was a road all right, and indeed went along the river, but was certainly not great).

But little old men who don't do much of anything except rock and watch passing vehicles eventually grow weary of such a humdrum life. So on a February morning, when a cool winter breeze blew north from the Gulf of Mexico, one little old man rose from his rocking chair and tottered down the porch steps to the house next door.

"Hey dere, Dumbo!" he shouted.

"Hey, Bubby," Dumbo answered. (His real name was Armand Boudreaux, which is a good Cajun name, but Cajuns keep their childhood nicknames throughout their lives. That's why you might meet a dignified gentleman wearing a suit and tie who will introduce himself as Stinky.)

"You passin' a good time?" Bubby shouted.

"I can't complain, me," Dumbo replied. "Come see."

So Bubby struggled up the steps and sat down next to his friend.

"You wanta play some bouree, Dumbo?" bellowed Bubby, who was pretty deaf, especially when he didn't want to listen. (You should know at this point that bouree is a Cajun card game, sort of a combination of bridge, poker, and hog-calling.)

"Has a possum got a tail?" Dumbo replied. (That's how Cajuns say "yes.") "But we can't play no bouree 'cept we get some mo' fellas."

So Bubby and Dumbo ambled down the road a bit and called on two more of their friends, Cap Hebert (pronounced Ay-bear) and Rigger Moritz (pronounced Rigor Mortis). They, too, were tired of rocking and ready for a lively game.

They decided to play at Bubby's home, since he was the one who thought of the idea. Actually, it was the home of his daughter and her husband and children. Bubby lived with them. (Cajuns are very nice to their aging parents.)

The four little old men set up a card table in the living room and began to play. Sometimes Bubby's daughter would look in on them and smile. She was glad to see her father and his friends doing something besides sitting and rocking—especially since her father's rocking chair creaked so loudly.

Now, bouree is a noisy game. For one thing, it's played by Cajuns, and Cajuns can get a little rowdy. For another thing, you just can't play bouree without hooting and hollering. This is why Bubby's daughter quickly stopped smiling so much and asked them to play more quietly. The four little old men were astonished by this, for everyone knew it was impossible for Cajuns to be quiet when playing bouree.

The playing continued, but Bubby's home grew louder and louder. Finally Bubby's daughter told the four little old men to play bouree somewhere else. So off they went to Cap Hebert's house. His wife was kind—and almost completely deaf, so hooting and hollering didn't bother her a bit. Thus, the rest of winter passed peacefully for all, except for Cap's cat and dog, who spent their days hiding under the house.

But when spring arrived, the four little old men began to feel restless. They could hear mockingbirds singing outside and tugboats on the river. Through the windows they could see bald cypress trees and willow trees turning green and sac-a-lait jumping in the canal. The spring air in Cap's house was as fresh as ever, but to the four little old men it seemed stale and thick.

"Oh, me," moaned Rigger Moritz. "It shore does look nice on de outside."

"What?" Bubby yelled.

"He says it looks nice outside," said Dumbo. "Seems a lil stuffy in here. No offense, Cap."

"Dat's okay. It *is* stuffy. A body can't hardly breathe in here," Cap replied.

That's when Bubby had his second great idea. "Why don' we move outside awhile?" he shouted.

Everyone was amazed at Bubby's clever suggestion, especially since he wasn't nearly as clever at bouree. The four little old men folded up the card table and chairs and lugged them across the Great River Road until they found a nice spot under a huge oak tree. And there, at the bottom of the Mississippi River levee, they set up the bouree game once again.

Every day, all day, they played cards around their table under the oak tree, enjoying the wind blowing on their bald and gray heads and the sounds of huge ships passing by them. People driving down the Great River Road smiled at them, and their fame spread near and far.

Of course, nothing in life is perfect. When it rained, the four little old men had to rush back across the road with their table and chairs. They were so slow that by the time the four little soaking wet men made it to Cap's porch, the rainstorm had often already come and gone.

"Whoooee!" Dumbo said, after one of these unpleasant experiences. "I'm soaking to my skin, an dat's de truth!"

As they stood shivering, watching a rainbow form in the sky, Bubby was strangely silent. Then he spoke, quietly for once, as if he were talking to himself. (That's because he was talking to himself.) "Shore we could," he said. "We could do it."

"Do what, Bubby?" Dumbo asked.

"What?" Bubby shouted back.

"What could we do?" repeated Dumbo.

"Build a roof!" Bubby hollered.

And that's just what they did.

Dumbo and Rigger rode in Dumbo's pick-em-up truck (that's Cajun for pickup truck) to the lumberyard, while Cap walked over to the hardware store to buy some nails. Bubby supplied a piece of moldy tarp that he'd stored years ago "just in case." And over the next week, in spite of many arguments, they built a shaky roof frame supported on four posts, with Bubby's tarp nailed on top.

Right through the summer they played bouree under their shelter, safe from the rain. Well, maybe not completely safe. The canvas kept off a light rain nicely, but in a heavy downpour it leaked. Strong winds made the tarp flap and the entire structure sway. And rainwater ran off the levee, flowing right through the grass under their feet.

The four little old men had to make their shelter stronger. They built a floor raised up above the wet grass, and they added a plywood roof and covered it with the tarp. Yet they were still all wet when the heavy rains came.

After putting up with the soggy shack for several months, the four little old men decided to fix the problem once and for all. They removed the tarp and covered the roof with shingles. It took two weeks to finish the job because there was only one ladder. (Also, they were very slow.) But the day the roof was completed, there was a big celebration, with lemonade and sarsaparilla.

For the rest of that year, when passersby saw the four little old men sitting under their shingled roof by the side of the road, they would wave and honk. The men would always be sure to honk back, even if they were concentrating on the bouree game. Life was sweet.

That is, until the cold weather came.

Winter's bitter wind blew straight through the shaky little shelter, scattering cards onto the floor. The cold made the bones of the four little old men creak like Bubby's rocking chair.

Tired of suffering through bad weather, the men built plywood walls. After the walls were up, they cut windows for light and a door on the north side.

But the wind and rain could still blow into their bouree game through the doorway and the window holes. So they bought a nice wooden door at the hardware store and five glass windowpanes. Now they could close the door and the windows against the wind, yet still see the passing world outside.

The four little old men were so proud of all these improvements that they forgot about bouree for a while. They simply stood back and admired their wonderful little house under the spreading oak tree.

"Looky here, fellas," said Cap. "Les make dis real nice, yeah. Les paint it." The men spent several pleasant days arguing about what color to use. Then Rigger found several old cans of purple paint that his wife, for some reason, had not allowed him to use on their dining room walls, and the question was settled.

The painting took several days. When it was done, not only was the house purple, but also the grass, the trunk of the oak tree, and the four little old men.

"Dat's beeeotiful," breathed Dumbo.

By this time, they'd almost forgotten how to play bouree. But now that the little house looked fine enough to suit them, they started their game up again.

Bubby's daughter brought two flower boxes and nailed them under the windows that faced the Great River Road. Then she planted pansies and begonias and snapdragons. "There!" she exclaimed. "Now that's the best-looking bouree house in all of Louisiana!"

And people driving along the Great River Road admired the house. Sometimes, if the angle was right, they could actually see the four little old men through a window, making the playing cards fly.

This very fine situation continued until about the middle of November. As almost always happens, the days had been getting shorter and shorter as winter approached. One day in late afternoon, just as the game was getting interesting, Dumbo said, "Durn! I can't hardly see de cards."

"Whooee!" Rigger yelled. "Dat's a relief. I thought I wus goin blind!"

"Looky here," cried Rigger. "It's getting too dark in here to play bouree."

"Wut we gonna do?" asked Dumbo. "Bouree's getting too good to stop now."

After the question was repeated to Bubby, he looked around the table and said, "There's only one thing to do. We got to get some electricity in here."

For once, they all fell silent. How were they supposed to get electricity? There was no electricity on the levee side of the Great River Road. But Bubby saved the day, as usual. "Listen!" he yelled excitedly. "I tell you wut we do."

Two days later a pick-em-up truck pulled in next to the little bouree house. Two strong young men got out and unloaded an electric generator, which they mounted on a wooden platform behind the house. Then an electrician came out and began drilling holes and running wires. In three days, the house had not only lights with wall switches, but also electrical outlets so the little old men could make coffee or plug in a radio. All through the winter, the people passing on the Great River Road could see lights shining through the windows of the house as the old men played their endless game.

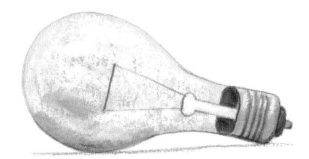

But a strange thing happened when spring rolled around. Maybe you can guess what it was. As the days grew longer and warmer, the four little old men began to feel restless again. Through the windows they could see the cypress trees and the willows turning green, but they could no longer see the sac-a-lait swimming in the canal. The air in the little house seemed stale and thick.

"What do you think, Dumbo?" said Cap. "Can we open the windows?"

"It's getting a lil stuffy in here, for shore," added Rigger Moritz.

They all trooped out and set up the table and chairs in the grass on the other side of the oak tree. And there, in the open air, the bouree game continued through the spring, summer, fall, and even winter. They bought a plastic table and chairs that were good in any kind of weather.

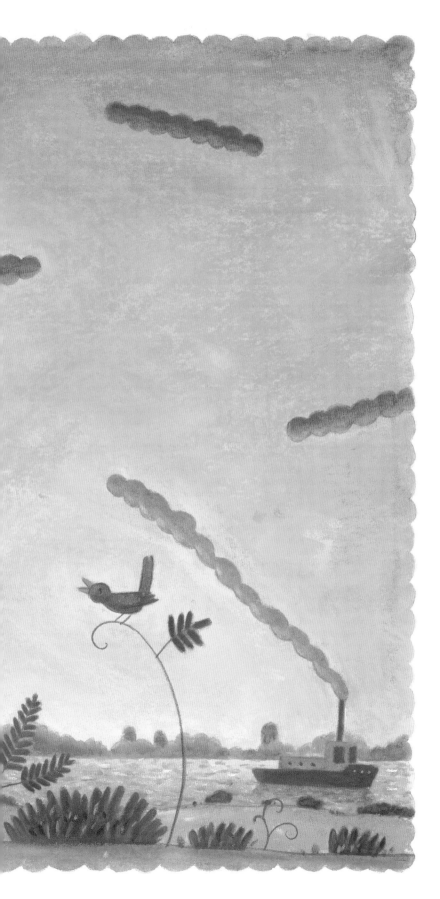

In a light rain, they would wear their raincoats and go right on with the game. In a heavy rain, they might step into their little house until it passed, then return to the outside world of tree frogs and crickets and cicadas. When cold winds blew, they'd bundle up in their winter clothes and pull on their gloves with the fingers cut off so they could still hold the cards. Their shouts and laughs echoed across the levee. The frogs croaked, the mockingbirds made up new songs, and the sac-a-lait splashed in the canal. The passing ships hooted, the breezes played rustling melodies in the oak leaves, and the people in the passing cars and trucks waved and smiled.

But the best-looking bouree house in all of Louisiana sat empty, slowly going to ruin, until one day people passing by on the Great River Road noticed that someone had torn it down.

But the four little old men never noticed it was gone.